The Adventures of Ollie and Polly

ISBN 978-1-0980-6737-3 (paperback)
ISBN 978-1-68517-062-2 (hardcover)
ISBN 978-1-0980-6738-0 (digital)

Christian Faith Publishing, Inc.
832 Park Avenue
Meadville, PA 16335
www.christianfaithpublishing.com

Printed in the United States of America

The Adventures of Ollie and Polly

A Day at the Zoo

Keri Johnson

Ollie and Polly are the best of friends,
When they're together, the fun never ends!

Each time they play, new adventures await,
It is so much fun to see the memories they create.

Today's adventure is a trip to the zoo,
They'll see so many animals by the time they are through!

Come along with us, and let's play a game,
At the end of their journey, let's see how many you can name!

Ollie and Polly walked into the zoo,
They saw so many animals yellow, orange, and blue.

They smelled the food baking and heard the other kids laughing,
They saw some kids riding in wagons and some were even walking.

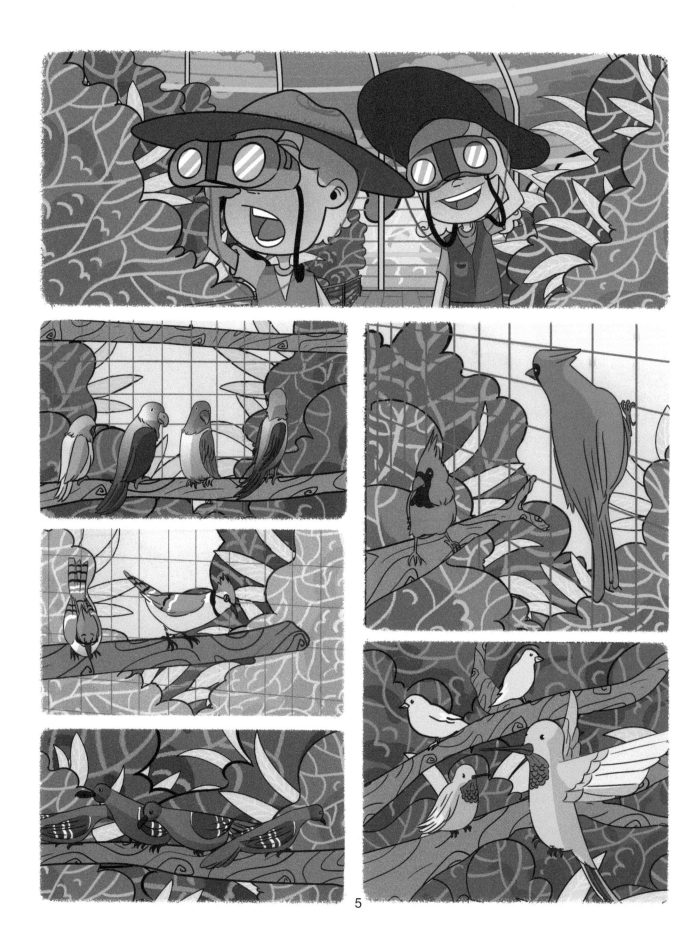

When they wandered through the displays of the colorful birds,
They were singing the prettiest songs they had ever heard.

The melody was smooth and soft, and very very sweet,
It was so simple and soothing going *tweet, tweet, tweet*!

Ollie and Polly saw some more birds,
And one had such a funny name it was hard to say the word.

Each time they tried, they just laughed and laughed,
They hadn't seen something this funny since they saw the giraffes!

In order to say it, they had to take it very, very slow,
This bashful bird was known as the Dodo!

8

They got to see the swans all peaceful and white,
And they waited anxiously for one to take flight.

They wanted to see it fly and spread its wings,
And they were curious to see what songs they would sing.

But it was time to move on and go see something new,
There were so many more animals to see here at the zoo!

They saw a beautiful checkered cheetah lounging in the sun,
And another playing with a ball having so much fun.

Ollie and Polly gazed at the lion who sat perched on his mound,
They even got to see kangaroos bouncing up and down.

They watched the water ripple from the
strides of the great green gators,
Amazed at all of this beauty designed by our Creator.

"What has been your favorite today, Polly?" asked Ollie.
"Mine has been the funny flamingos."

"For me, Ollie," started Polly,
"I enjoyed seeing the huge hungry hippos!"

14

So much to see and so much to learn,
Making sure to apply their sunscreen to not get burned.

Ollie and Polly took in all the sights,
And they even got to see two elks fight!

Their horns were locked, and their faces were fierce,
Ollie and Polly hoped they weren't hurt and didn't have any tears.

They explored the exotic elephants and their elaborate trunks,
Felling the ground vibrate as their feet went *clunk, clunk, clunk!*

The magical monkeys swung from limb to limb,
And the gorilla made a fresh nest to lie down in.

But up next was the part they had been looking forward to the most,
They had only seen this kind of water from on top of a boat.

They wandered through the aquatic display and saw a stunning sea otter,
They were mesmerized by the octopus and its tentacles moving him around the water.

They counted the colors of the coral reef and saw all the little fish,
They even got to see a shark with its fin cutting the water going *swish, swish, swish*!

In another habitat, the penguins pranced proudly along the slippery ledge,
They dove, and they swam, and they got back up on the ice wedge.

The space was cold and a lot of it dark,
Ollie and Polly wondered how Noah kept all of them warm on the ark.

Two by two, they knew they all came aboard,
Each and every animal made by the Lord.

They wondered how animals with such different needs
Could all be together under one roof in peace.

They were grateful for Noah and his family and all they sacrificed,
And that they followed the calling of the plan God had devised.

Across the park and around the bend,
Ollie headed to the concession stand with his friend.

They took a break before heading back out,
Then "Oh my gosh!" Ollie heard Polly shout.

Ollie turned his head and saw a snake slithering close,
Hissing and hissing and both Ollie and Polly froze.

There was no need to be afraid, they were safe as could be,
There was no way the snake could slither and break free.

"Hey, Ollie, I am getting tired," Polly said with a yawn.
"Me too," replied Ollie, "but before we go, I want to go back to see the swans."

One last time, they wanted to stand and stare,
Wondering if they would get to see one take off in the air.

Just as they went to leave, one started to fly,
A snow-white swan extended its wings and took off toward the sky.

They headed together back toward the front gate,
They would have to see the rest of the animals on another date.

On the way home, they recounted all the fun they had had,
And when it came time to say goodbye, they got a little sad.

"Bye, Polly!" shouted Ollie.
"Thank you for coming with me to the zoo!"

"Bye, Ollie!" replied Polly.
"Remember, God made all those beautiful creatures, and he made us too!"

About the Author

Keri Johnson always had an active imagination growing up, acting out thoroughly planned story lines while exploring her surroundings. In sixth grade, she put one of those stories on paper that ignited her desire for writing. With the encouragement of her parents, she pursued writing throughout school and decided on a career in education to help teach others what she was so passionate about and the power a story can have. She knew her dream was to write professionally and share her stories with others, and for years, Keri tossed around ideas, trying to decide on one that was worth publishing. When she became a mother and was able to watch as her children grew in curiosity and creativity, she realized her greatest responsibility as a mother. She wanted to publish a book, and ultimately a series, of children exploring the world around them, asking questions, and learning about the amazing creations and unconditional love of our God. She wants to leave her children a legacy using her passion to share her faith with the world, and as a result, *The Adventures of Ollie and Polly* were born.

CPSIA information can be obtained
at www.ICGtesting.com
Printed in the USA
BVHW021331250122
627121BV00006B/236